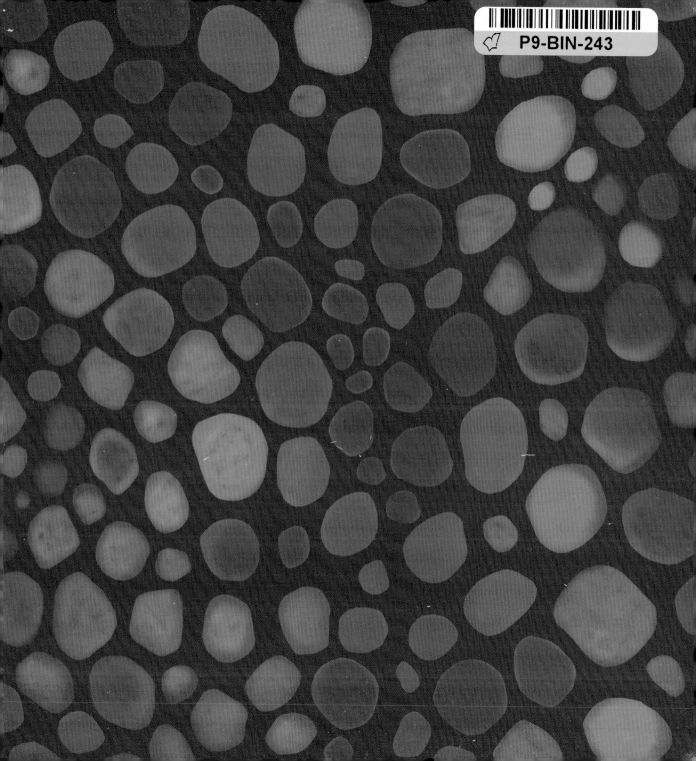

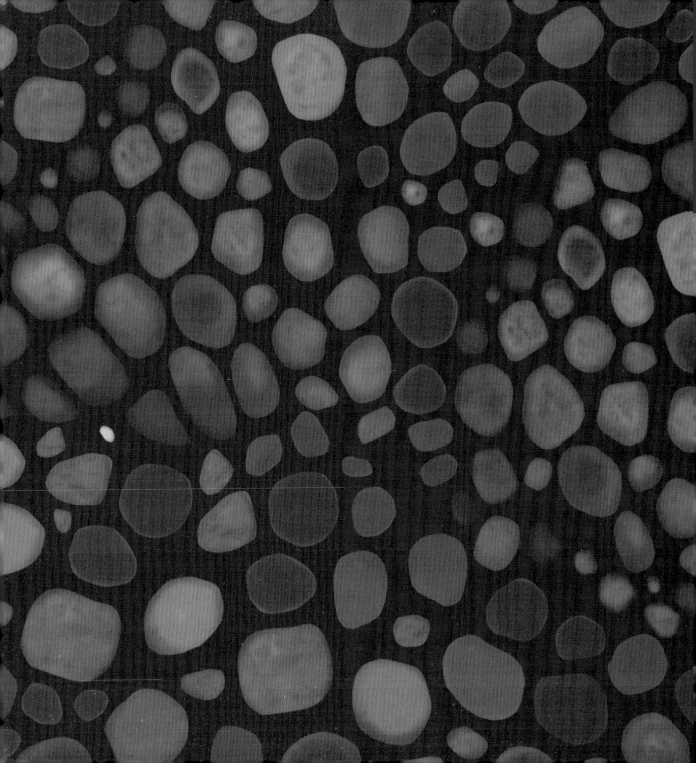

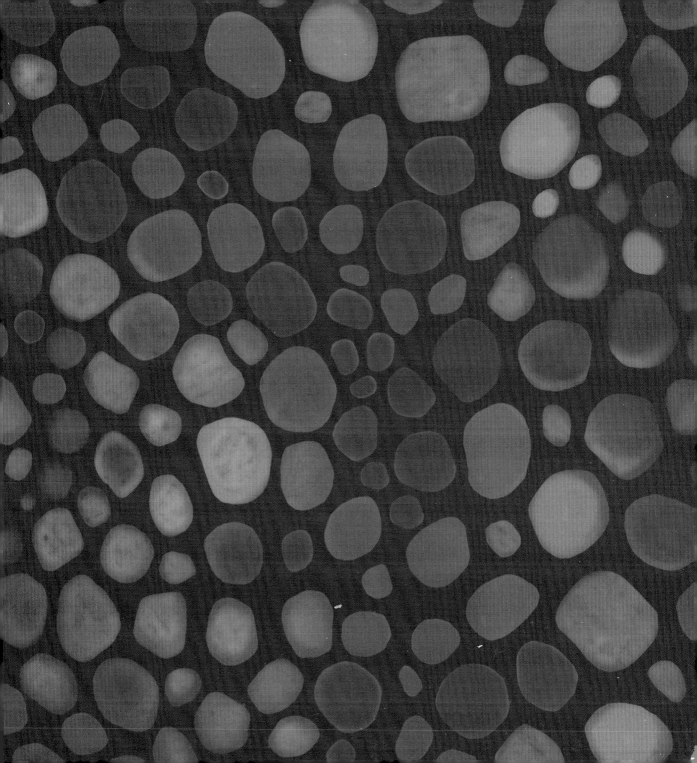

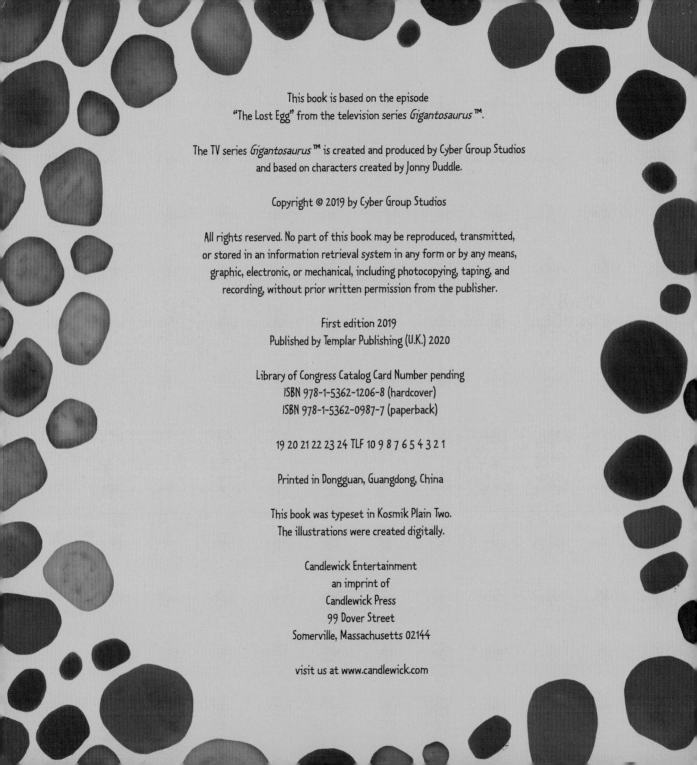

This book is based on the episode
"The Lost Egg" from the television series *Gigantosaurus* ™.

The TV series *Gigantosaurus* ™ is created and produced by Cyber Group Studios
and based on characters created by Jonny Duddle.

First edition 2019
Published by Templar Publishing (U.K.) 2020

Library of Congress Catalog Card Number pending
ISBN 978-1-5362-1206-8 (hardcover)
ISBN 978-1-5362-0987-7 (paperback)

19 20 21 22 23 24 TLF 10 9 8 7 6 5 4 3 2 1

Printed in Dongguan, Guangdong, China

This book was typeset in Kosmik Plain Two.
The illustrations were created digitally.

Candlewick Entertainment
an imprint of
Candlewick Press
99 Dover Street
Somerville, Massachusetts 02144

visit us at www.candlewick.com

GIGANTOSAURUS™

THE LOST EGG

CANDLEWICK
ENTERTAINMENT

It was a warm, sunny day in the Cretaceous world. Rocky, Tiny, Bill, and Mazu were scampering up and down the jungle trails, playing a game of Giganto Tag. It was Bill's turn. After a little while, he spotted Tiny hiding behind a rock and ran toward her.

Tiny roared, doing her very best Gigantosaurus impression, then raced off to tag Mazu.

As soon as the coast was clear, Rocky jumped out of his hiding place. "No one can catch me. I'm a super dino!" he said, running away as fast as he could.

But Rocky wasn't looking where he was going. His foot got tangled in a vine, sending him tumbling down the path — straight into a shiny EGG. He picked it up.

Huh?!
What's this?

"Look what I found!" Rocky called out, spinning the egg on his finger as the others rushed over.

"What's an egg doing here?" said Mazu. "There's no nest around."

"We have to take care of it!" urged Tiny. "Remember, there's a baby dino inside."

Rocky snorted. That didn't sound fun at all.

"That's not a job for a super-tough dino like me," he replied. "Why don't we just leave it here and get back to our game?"

You have to be gentle!

Rocky's friends were worried about the lost egg. What kind of dinosaur was inside? Who were its parents? Would it be safe out here alone?

Just as Rocky tried to leave the egg and get back to the game of Giganto Tag, a thunderous noise came rumbling toward them.

The earth shook as a herd of ENORMOUS triceratops charged past the little dinos, kicking up a cloud of dust.

"We can't leave the egg here," said Mazu. "It might get crushed!"

Tiny agreed and scooped the egg into her arms. "We're going to find your family," she said. "I promise."

"Fine," huffed Rocky. "But let's hurry up so we can get back to having fun. I'm WAY TOO TOUGH to be looking after a SILLY LITTLE EGG!"

After walking in the jungle for a while, the dinosaurs spotted their friend Archie perched high up on a rock.

Is this egg yours?

Archie swooped down to get a closer look, knocking Rocky to the ground.

The dinos walked all morning, but they couldn't find the egg's family.

"This is taking forever," grumbled Rocky. "We'll never have time to finish our game if we don't move faster!"

He grabbed the egg and darted through the trees. Then he tripped AGAIN! This time he fell straight into Ignatius.

"You didn't happen to lose an egg?" Rocky asked the little yellow dinosaur.

"That egg's almost as big as me!" Ignatius said.

Rocky and his friends went to see every dinosaur they could think of. They asked spiky ones and scaly ones, stompy ones and slithery ones, but the lost egg didn't belong to any of them.

They ventured a little deeper into the forest to see Rugo the rat, but it definitely wasn't hers. She just laughed.

"Lucky mammals!" groaned Rocky, stomping away.
"Eggs are nothing but trouble."

The dinos were tired and thirsty. Luckily, Rocky knew just what to do.

"Coconut milk, coming right down!" he shouted. He shook a tree and one by one the coconuts fell to the ground, nearly squashing the egg each time!

The others rushed to protect the egg.

"Why do you all care so much? It's not like the egg cares about us!" Rocky snapped. But at that moment, it rolled across the grass, up to Rocky's feet. Maybe it DID care.

"The egg seems to like you, Rocky!" said Tiny.

"Hmm . . ." muttered Rocky, looking at the little egg. "Do you think this thing actually has feelings?"

The friends passed Ayati, who was grazing in the sunshine.

"Did you lose this egg?" asked Rocky.

"No," said Ayati, "but I can incubate it for you."

What does "incubate" mean?

It means sitting on an egg to keep it warm.

Ayati took the egg from Rocky and got ready to lower her enormous body onto it.

"NO!" shouted Rocky, grabbing the egg just before she squashed it.

"Ayati," said Mazu, "I'm not sure that dino eggs have to be incubated!"

The little dinos walked down to the lake.

"Who do you belong to, Eggsy?" asked Tiny, laughing as she gave it a pretty flower hat. "We've asked nearly every dinosaur we know!"

Eggsy looks so cute!

SPLASH! A huge shape rose out of the water. Terminonator!

"Hello, little dinos. I see you've found my egg," she said, drooling.
"I've been craving one for BREAKFAST all morning."

Terminonator lunged toward the little dinos. Grasping
the egg tightly, Rocky and his friends sprinted away, escaping
the huge toothy jaws just in time!

"Don't worry, little egg," said Rocky, hurrying away from the lake. "I'll protect you."

"Aw," cooed Tiny. "That's so cute!"

"Only because SOMEBODY has to," said Rocky in his toughest voice. He looked back down at the egg, which seemed to be shaking.

UH-OH!

The others looked around. The egg wasn't shaking. It was the ground! That could only mean one thing . . .

"GIGANTOSAURUS!"

The enormous dinosaur stomped over, lowered his head, and picked up the egg in his teeth!

"He's going to EAT it!" shouted Tiny. "I can't watch!"

But Giganto didn't eat it. He carefully placed the egg on a mound of mud, then settled down beside it for a nap.

Rocky couldn't believe his eyes. He'd never seen a fierce dinosaur be so gentle.

Hmm, thought Rocky. *If Giganto isn't embarrassed to show his soft side, maybe I don't have to be, either. . . .*

At that moment, the friends heard a cracking sound.
The egg was HATCHING!

A teeny-tiny dinosaur popped its head out of the shell and smiled up at them.
It had red scales and a little head crest.

"Look!" gasped Rocky. "It's a baby parasaurolophus. Just like me!"

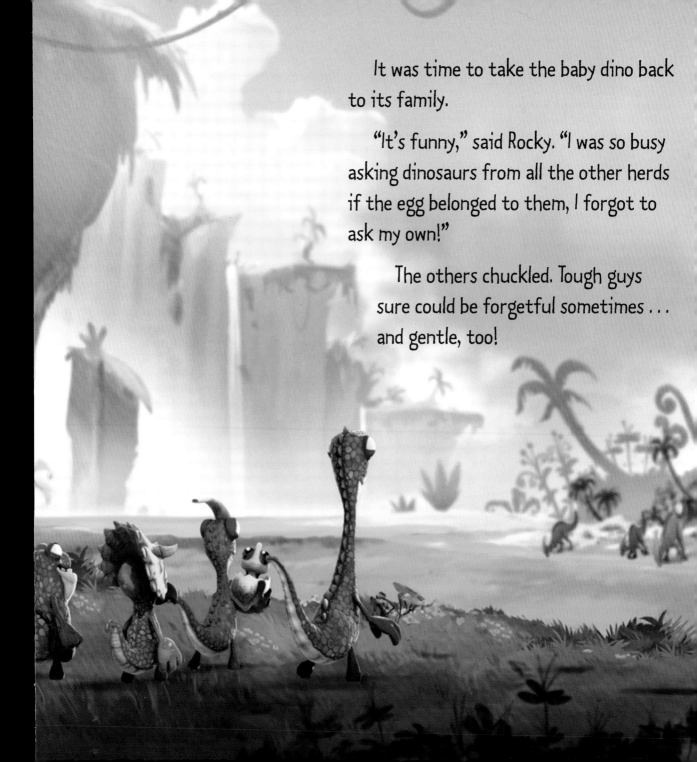

It was time to take the baby dino back to its family.

"It's funny," said Rocky. "I was so busy asking dinosaurs from all the other herds if the egg belonged to them, I forgot to ask my own!"

The others chuckled. Tough guys sure could be forgetful sometimes . . . and gentle, too!

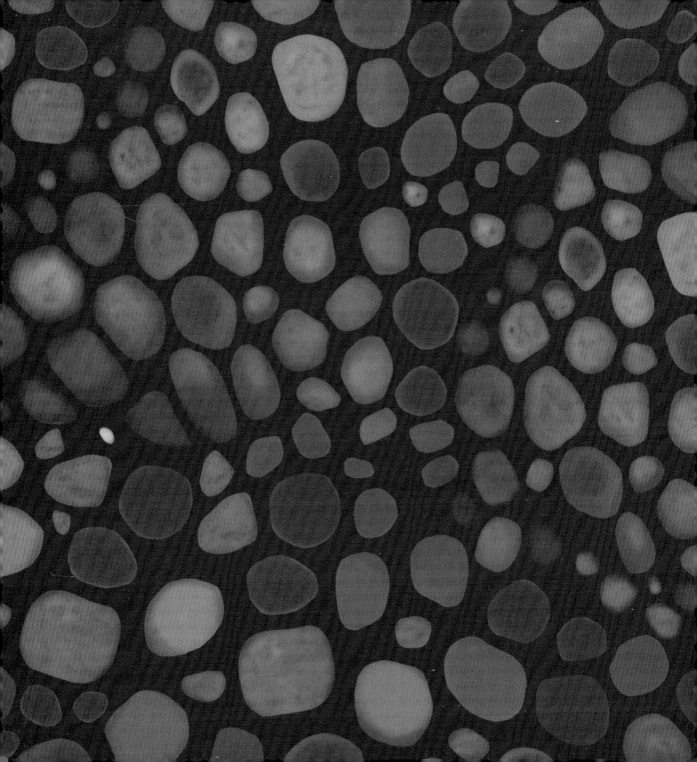

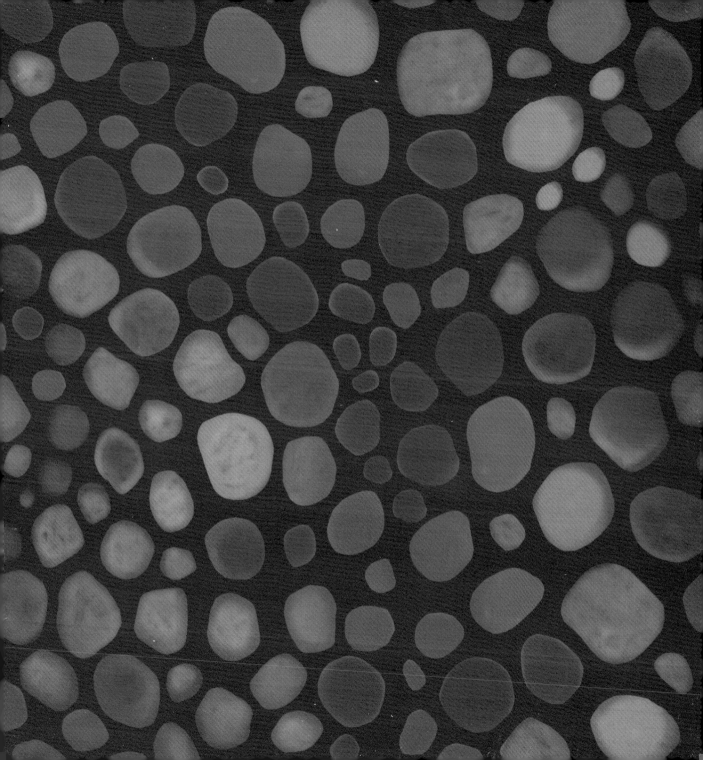

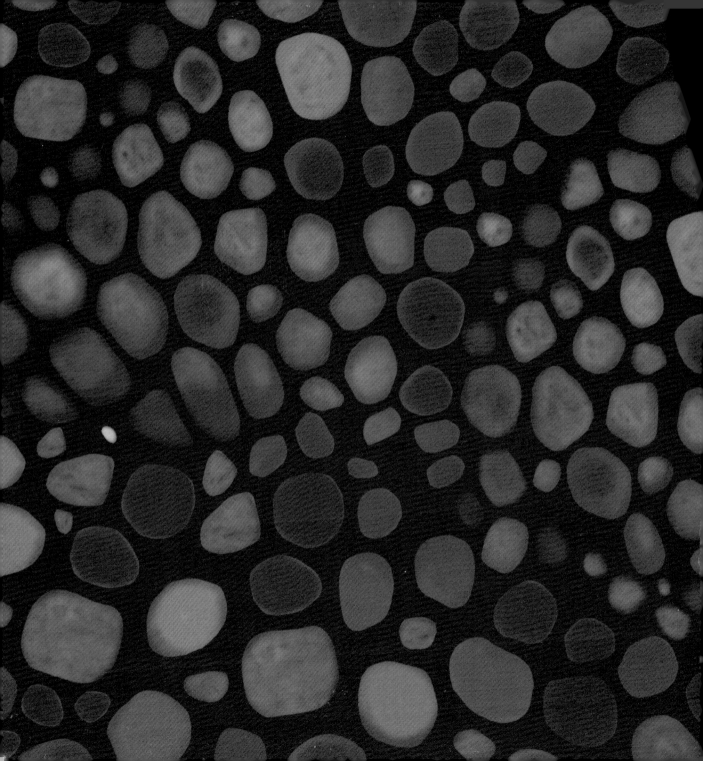

GIGANTOSAURUS